SCOOBY-DOO!
And The LEGEND OF THE VAMPIRE

Adapted by Jenny Markas from the script by Mark E. Turosz

SCHOLASTIC INC.
New York   Toronto   London   Auckland   Sydney
Mexico City   New Delhi   Hong Kong   Buenos Aires

Visit Scholastic.com for information
about our books and authors online!

ISBN 0-439-45521-9

Designed by Louise Bova

12 11 10 9 8 7 6 5 4 3 2 1   3 4 5 6 7 8/0

Special thanks to Duendes del Sur for insert illustrations

Printed in the U.S.A.
First printing, March 2003

For Holly

Chapter 1

"**L**ike, this is going to be the best vacation ever!" Shaggy said, looking over the most fantastic spread of food he'd ever seen. There was turkey and ham and fried chicken, lobster and shrimp, cakes and pies, and five kinds of cookies.

"Ruh-huh!" agreed Scooby, licking his chops.

Scooby and the gang were on their way to Australia, the land down under, home to koalas, kangaroos, and awesome beaches. Best of all, the vacation had already started, since they were traveling there on board a huge cruise ship.

While Scooby and Shaggy loaded up four towering plates each, Daphne climbed up to the diving board, bounced a few times, and did a cannonball into the pool. The splash was so huge, it drenched the shuffleboard court, where Velma and Fred were playing.

"Great form, Daphne!" Velma said sarcastically.

"I'll say," agreed Fred, wringing water from his shirt.

Shaggy carried his plate of sandwiches stacked up

tall to the table where Scooby was sitting. Scooby looked down at his own small pizza, then looked jealously at his friend's plate. Then he had an idea. He tossed his pizza through the air like a boomerang. It whizzed by Shaggy, picking up *all* of his sandwiches, before making its way back to Scooby, who ate it in a single gulp.

"Hey!" Shaggy said.

Scooby just giggled.

Just then, Velma spoke up. "Hey, everybody! Come take a look!" She was standing over by the railing. Everybody joined her and gazed out into the distance. "It's Sydney Harbour!" said Velma, pointing to a beautiful city on a big, sweeping bay.

"Wow!" said Fred. "We're finally in Australia."

"This is going to be the best vacation ever!" exclaimed Daphne.

"Ruh-huh!" Scooby agreed.

The ship moved into the harbor and docked at a long pier. By the time the ramp was set up, the gang was ready to go.

"What vacation would be complete without the Mystery Machine?" asked Fred proudly as the multicolored van was lowered to the dock below.

The gang was all set for their awesome Australian vacation.

Chapter 2

Meanwhile, deep in the Australian outback . . .

Daniel Illiwara and his grandfather Malcolm were watching some workers set up lights and amplifiers on a big outdoor stage. VAMPIRE ROCK MUSIC FESTIVAL, read a colorful banner hung across the stage. In the background was an enormous rock formation that rose high and wide from the dusty, level ground around it. It was known as Vampire Rock, and it looked like a strange, gigantic beast sitting hunched in the middle of the flat, scrubby outback.

"Just a little more to the left," Daniel called out, waving his hand as a worker adjusted a spotlight. "Perfect!" He checked his clipboard. There were a lot of details to take care of when you were organizing a concert.

Malcolm shook his head. He was a thin, elderly man who was proud of his Aboriginal heritage. He believed in all the spooky legends and ancient native tales about the strange things that can happen in the outback. "I'm telling you," he warned his grandson, "this concert is not a good idea."

"Relax, Grandfather. Everything will be fine." Daniel put an arm around Malcolm's shoulders. "C'mon," he said. "We're ready for Matt Marvelous's sound check. You'll love him."

Malcolm didn't look so sure. He gazed up at the young American rocker who was standing on stage, dressed in leather pants and a frilly velvet shirt. His long brown hair waved in the breeze as he strummed on his electric guitar.

Suddenly, Matt started playing a wild guitar solo. All the workers stopped what they were doing to watch and listen.

Daniel was grooving, too. "See?" he said to his grandfather. "This guy rocks!"

"If you say so," said Malcolm doubtfully. He looked like he was getting a headache.

"If he didn't rock," said Daniel, "he wouldn't be a finalist in the contest." He danced around, rocking out. But then, dark smoke started to billow up above the stage.

"What the . . . ?" Daniel asked, watching as the smoke moved down onto the stage. Electricity burst from the smoke — and it reached out and wrapped around Matt Marvelous.

"Wh–what's going on?" Matt stammered. He tried

to run off the stage, but the electricity surrounded him and lifted him into the air, toward a huge, hulking figure that stood almost a hundred feet tall.

"Let me go!" shrieked Matt. But the creature drew the musician toward him, cackling evilly. Then, as quickly as it had appeared, it was gone — and so was Matt.

Malcolm came up behind his grandson. They stood there looking up at the dark, smoky sky.

"The vampire legend is true," said Malcolm, shaking his head.

Chapter 3

Back in Sydney, Scooby and the gang were busy checking out Australia's biggest city. After some sightseeing and shopping, they hit Bondi Beach, the coolest beach in Sydney. Fred grilled some burgers while Velma read her guidebook in a beach chair, dressed in her usual turtleneck to protect her skin from the hot Australian sun. Shaggy and Scooby surfed the beautiful blue waves — until they got chased by a shark! Meanwhile, Daphne chatted with some cute lifeguards. She looked great in her purple-and-green bikini.

When the food was ready, the gang gathered to eat. Velma was still reading her guidebook. "How do you guys feel about exploring the outback?" she asked.

"Routback?" asked Scooby, exchanging a puzzled look with Shaggy.

"Sure," said Fred. "Australia's not all beach. The outback is the wild, inland part."

"Like, I know what the outback is," said Shaggy.

"And I don't want to go 'out back' to look at dust and trees."

"C'mon, Shaggy," Daphne said. "I'm sure there's more to see than that."

Velma held up her Polaroid camera. "And I've got seventeen rolls of film to capture it all!"

Fred was looking toward the boardwalk, where he spotted a big billboard. "What if you could hear great music while you were there?" he asked Shaggy. "At the Vampire Rock Music Festival." He pointed to the sign.

"That sounds like a lot of fun, Freddie," said Daphne.

Shaggy and Scooby looked at each other.

"Vampire?" asked Shaggy.

"Rampire?" echoed Scooby.

Velma checked her guidebook. "Vampire Rock is right in the middle of Australia," she said. "We can see a lot of the outback on our way there."

She sounded excited, but Shaggy shook his head. "Scooby and I don't think it's a good idea going to a place called Vampire Rock. That's asking for trouble."

"Reah," said Scooby, also shaking his head. "Rouble."

"That's just the name of the place," Fred told them.

Velma smiled. "There's no such thing as vampires," she said.

"I'm sure a festival that big will have every concession stand imaginable," Daphne said thoughtfully.

"Hamburgers," Shaggy said, "hot dogs, ice cream, popcorn — and probably some great local food, too!"

"Real music lovers," said Fred, rolling his eyes.

Shaggy and Scooby exchanged a glance. Then Shaggy shrugged. "Like, who ever heard of Australian vampires, anyway?" he asked.

Chapter 4

At Vampire Rock, Daniel's business partner, Russell, was arguing with Jasper Ridgeway, the manager of one of the bands that was going to play at the festival. Russell was a laid-back Aussie dude who had helped put on the original Vampire Rock Festival. Jasper had also been at the original Vampire Rock Festival, as Wildwind's manager. Jasper was trying to get Russell to give the Bad Omens, the goth band he now managed, more time on stage.

"For the last time," Russell said, "every contestant gets three minutes."

"But," whined Jasper, "the Bad Omens' best song lasts *five* minutes."

"Rules are rules," said Russell, folding his arms.

"Can't you bend the rules for such an upstanding group of young people?" begged Jasper.

Russell looked over at the Bad Omens, slouching nearby. All three were dressed in black from head to toe.

King, the singer, looked impatient. "This better be important," he said. "I've got things to pierce."

The drummer, Jack, held up a mirror and stared into it. "And I'm trying to find a new shade of eyeliner," he added.

Queen, the bass player, just cracked her gum and blew an enormous bubble.

The Bad Omens did not exactly look like upstanding young people.

"You were saying?" Russell asked Jasper.

"C'mon, Russell," Jasper pleaded. "Now that Matt Marvelous is gone, it's obvious the Bad Omens are the best in the contest. Why not just declare us the winner now?"

King, Queen, and Jack seemed to think that was a great idea.

But Russell didn't like it one bit. "Jasper, get out of my face or the Bad Omens won't perform at all!" he said.

Jasper wouldn't back down. "You're making a big mistake, Russell. I didn't have to come back here, especially after what happened to Wildwind last year. But I am back. And I intend to have my group win this time."

Russell stared back at him. "I'm warning you . . ." he said.

Jasper just grunted and walked back toward the

Bad Omens. "Let's get out of here," he told them. They stalked out, passing Daniel on their way off-stage.

Daniel came out to join Russell. "Jasper's never going to get over what happened to Wildwind," Daniel said, shaking his head. He and Russell looked over at a blown-up poster of Wildwind, performing at last year's festival. "Even if it *has* been a whole year since they disappeared."

"From what you told me about last night," said Russell, "it sounds like they're making a comeback. Maybe it's true about Wildwind turning into vampires."

"Come on," said Daniel. "That's just a local myth."

"So what do you think happened to Matt Marvelous, then?" asked Russell. "You saw the vampires with your own two eyes."

Daniel frowned. "I don't know what I saw, Russell," he answered.

"Well," Russell told him, "the crew's looked all over Vampire Rock. There's no sign of Matt or the vampires."

Daniel turned his gaze to the massive rock looming over the barren landscape. He shivered, as if a chill had gone down his spine. "Maybe Grandfather was right," he murmured. "Maybe we should postpone the festival."

Russell was staring at the rock, too. He had a worried look in his eyes. "No way," he said. "We've both worked too hard to quit now, Daniel."

"I know," said Daniel. "The show must go on. But this kidnapping makes me nervous, Russell. Very nervous."

The partners stood quietly, gazing at the rock.

Chapter 5

As Fred drove the Mystery Machine through the unbounded expanse of the outback, Shaggy looked out the window and sighed. "Like I said," he complained, "nothing but dust and trees."

Velma shook her head. "You'd be surprised, Shaggy," she told him. "The outback is full of life."

"Like, I'll believe it when I see it," said Shaggy.

Sure enough, as the gang drove farther into the wild center of Australia, they saw the most amazing things. When they stopped for a picnic, a red-tailed parrot stole a Scooby Snack right out of Scooby's paw. Shaggy and Scooby had a hopping contest with some kangaroos. A slithery brown king snake scared Scooby out of his wits when it wrapped itself around a football the gang was playing with. Some wildcats chased Scooby away from a stream where he was getting a drink. A bearded dragon lizard stuck out his tongue at the gang. And some galloping, wingless emus charged Shaggy and Scooby, chasing them right into the van. It was a wild trip.

Finally, just as night was beginning to fall, Fred took the turn marked VAMPIRE ROCK. When the monumental rock came into view, the whole gang gasped.

"There it is," said Velma. "Vampire Rock."

"Wow," said Fred.

"It's spectacular!" said Daphne.

Velma opened up her laptop and hit some keys. Soon a picture of Vampire Rock showed up on the screen. "It says the locals call it Vampire Rock because they believe the Yowie Yahoo lives in the rock's caves," Velma read.

Daphne looked confused. "The Yowie Yahoo?"

Velma nodded. "It's an ancient Australian vampire."

Shaggy's jaw dropped. "Zoinks!" he said. "We were wrong, Scoob. There *are* Australian vampires."

Velma hit another key and the printer set up next to her started to hum. In a moment, it spit out a full-color picture of the Yowie Yahoo. It was a terrifying creature, twenty feet tall and bulging with muscles. It looked sort of human, except for its glowing red eyes, glistening fangs, and pale white skin.

Shaggy picked it up and showed it to Scooby. "Next time I agree to go to a place named after a vampire, I need you to do me a favor, Scoob. Like, talk me out of it!"

It was dark outside by the time the Mystery Machine pulled up at the concert site. The place was deserted.

"Are we in the right spot?" Daphne asked.

"Uh-huh," said Fred. "This is it."

The gang trooped out of the van and started toward the campsite. Scooby brought up the rear. But he turned around when he heard the sound of growling in the bushes . . . and then saw a pair of glowing eyes! He grabbed Shaggy's arms and pointed at the bushes.

"What is it, Scoob?" Shaggy peered at the bushes, but there was nothing there. "Like, very funny Scoob. You almost had me going there."

As soon as Shaggy turned around again the Yowie Yahoo burst from behind the bushes. He was taller than the trees and twice as terrifying as his picture! Scooby ran away as fast as he could — and jumped right on Shaggy's shoulders.

"Like, what is it now?" Shaggy asked. Then he saw it, too. "Zoinks! It's the Yowie Yahoo!"

"Where?" asked Fred.

"I already told you guys, there's no such thing as vampires," said Velma.

"Then what's that noise?" asked Shaggy.

The gang listened, and everybody heard something moving around. Footsteps . . . twigs snapping . . . leaves rustling . . .

"Like, those are sounds I don't want to hear," Shaggy said, looking scared.

"Ruh-huh," agreed Scooby, jumping into Shaggy's arms.

"Whatever it is," Fred said, "it's coming closer."

"Do something, Freddie!" cried Daphne.

Fred shone his flashlight into the trees. Two bright red eyes glowed back at them, lit up by the light of the beam.

"Zoinks!" yelled Shaggy. "It's the vampire!" He dropped Scooby. Just then, a wild howling sound started up from another direction. The gang turned to look.

Up on some rocky cliffs not far away, three dingoes stood staring back at them with mysterious, greenish-yellow eyes.

"Jinkies," Velma gulped as the dingoes started down the cliffs. But the wild dogs ran right past the gang, toward a clump of trees. Fred shone his flashlight that way again, picking up the red eyes. When the dingoes started barking, the red eyes disappeared into the darkness.

"Do you hear that?" Daphne asked, cupping her hand around her ear. "Music." She started walking toward the stage. Velma turned around just long enough to snap a picture of the clump of trees. Then she ran to catch up.

When the gang got near the stage, they saw a familiar sight. "Hey, it's the Hex Girls!" called Daphne. It was their old friends up on stage: Thorn on vocals, Dusk playing drums, and Luna playing bass. The gang had met the world-famous rock trio while investigating a mystery back in the States.

"Like, I knew those tunes sounded familiar," said Shaggy. He smiled and waved.

Thorn stopped singing to take a closer look. "It *is* you!" she cried.

The gang walked up on stage. "Boy, are we glad to see you," Fred said, hugging Thorn until Daphne got jealous and elbowed him in the ribs.

"What are you doing here?" Dusk asked.

"Well, we were on vacation," Daphne began.

"And we thought we'd check out the festival," Fred finished.

"Cool!" Luna said. "We're the opening act!"

"How long have you guys been here?" Velma asked.

"A couple of days," Luna answered. "Why?"

"Have you seen anything strange since you arrived?" Velma asked.

"Like what?" Thorn asked.

"Like what?" Shaggy asked. "Like, how about big —"

Scooby rose up high, towering over Shaggy.

"And creepy —"

Scooby opened his eyes wide.

"And scary —"

Scooby held his arms over his head and started walking slowly toward the Hex Girls.

Just then, Daniel and Russell appeared. "I was wondering why the music stopped," said Daniel.

Chapter 6

Scooby dropped his arms, looking a little sheepish.

"We came over to make sure you were all right," Russell said to the Hex Girls.

Luna looked surprised. "Of course we're all right. Why wouldn't we be?"

"Just checking," said Russell. "Are you going to introduce us to your friends?"

Thorn nodded. "Sure! Daniel and Russell, these are our friends from America: Fred, Daphne, Velma, Shaggy —"

"Rand Rooby-Doo!" interrupted Scooby, putting out his paw to shake with both men.

"Well, g'day," said Russell. "We're the promoters of the festival."

"Welcome," said Daniel. "Sorry we interrupted. We're trying to clear up some trouble before the festival starts."

"What's going on?" Luna asked.

Daniel hesitated for a moment. "The finalists in

our unsigned band contest are disappearing," he admitted.

Daphne and Velma exchanged a look. "Well, that's not good," said Daphne.

Shaggy's eyes were wide. "Like, did you say — disappearing?"

Russell nodded.

Daniel shook his head. "Only now the groups are bailing out on us, as soon as they hear about Matt Marvelous being kidnapped. They go straight from 'g'day' to 'good-bye.'"

Fred stared at Daniel. "Kidnapped? By who?"

Shaggy thought he knew. "Like, maybe by those big, creepy, scary —"

"Vampires," somebody finished in a deep voice. Scooby jumped right into Shaggy's arms when he heard that!

It was Malcolm. He was climbing into his rattly old jeep, which was parked nearby. As he started it up, he spoke to Daniel. "I warned you terrible things would happen." Then he took off in a cloud of dust.

Shaggy stared after him. "Like, who was that spooky old man?"

"That was my grandfather," Daniel told him. "Malcolm Illiwara."

Shaggy blushed. "Oh. I meant spooky in a *good* way."

"You'll have to forgive him," Daniel said. "He's very upset."

Shaggy nodded. "Like, I understand. I'm pretty upset myself right now."

Velma was getting curious. "What did your grandfather mean by 'terrible things'?" she asked Daniel.

He looked straight at her and answered, "The Yowie Yahoo."

Shaggy looked up at Vampire Rock. "Zoinks!" he said. "Like, you mean the vampire who lives in there?"

"Right. Him and his minions, or at least so they say," said Daniel. "There's no such thing as vampires."

"Don't you mean *rock star* vampires?" Russell asked, facing the poster of Wildwind.

The Hex Girls turned to look. "Wow," said Dusk. "I've seen groups like Wildwind in my parents' record collection."

"Yeah, check out their makeup and costumes," said Luna.

"This poster must be from a long time ago," said Thorn.

"Nope," said Daniel, "They're just a few years older than you."

"Wildwind wanted to bring glam rock back," said Russell. "They had the most amazing stage show.

Dark Skull played guitar, Stormy Weathers played bass, and Lightning Strikes was on drums."

"So you saw them perform?" asked Daphne.

"I sure did," said Russell. "They deserved a lot better than third place in the contest."

"What happened to them?" asked Velma.

"After they lost the contest, they went up to Vampire Rock to rock climb and camp," Russell explained. "They were never heard from again."

Fred's jaw dropped. "They just disappeared?" he asked.

Daniel answered, "The locals believe that the Yowie Yahoo turned them into vampires."

Shaggy nodded wisely. "I'm with the locals. That would explain those big, creepy, scary —"

Scooby did his act again.

"All right, Shaggy," Daphne said. "We get your point."

"Anyway, there's no such thing as vampires," said Velma.

"Well, maybe not," said Russell. "But Daniel says he saw Matt Marvelous get kidnapped by three vampires who looked just like Wildwind."

"I never actually said vampires," Daniel pointed out. "But whoever or whatever they were, they were pretty convincing. Now I don't know what to think."

Shaggy was looking more frightened than ever.

"When did all this vampire stuff start, Daniel?" asked Velma.

"For as long as I can remember," Daniel told them, "there have been strange lights and sounds coming from Vampire Rock. My grandfather always told me it was the Yowie Yahoo. But I never believed him." He gazed up at the enormous rock looming in the distance. "I'd love to find out what's really going on up there."

Fred rubbed his hands together. "Well, gang," he said, "it looks like we have a mystery on our hands. And I think the best way to investigate is to go undercover as a rock band. If we're lucky, the Wildwind vampires will try to kidnap us next."

Shaggy looked at Scooby. "Like, I don't want to be that lucky!" he said.

"Ruh-uh," Scooby agreed.

But Daphne was ready. "That's a great idea, Freddie," she said.

Russell didn't seem so sure, but Daniel pointed out that it might be their only hope. "I guess it would work," Russell finally agreed. "Especially if it keeps my pick to win the contest from getting kidnapped."

"And who's that?" asked Daniel.

"Two Skinny Dudes," Russell said. "They're the real deal. You'll see when they get here."

"So, what do you say?" asked Fred.

"Well, okay," Russell agreed. "But don't say I didn't warn you."

"Scoob and I wouldn't mind sitting this one out," Shaggy said. "Like, maybe the group should be a trio."

But it was too late. The Hex Girls dragged Shaggy and Scooby backstage to dress them up like rock stars.

Meanwhile, a pair of glowing red eyes watched from a tree near the stage.

Chapter 7

Later, as a big yellow moon — nearly full — was rising, the gang showed up on stage again. Only this time, they looked different.

"I don't know how well we'll play," said Fred, "but at least we look the part." He gazed down at his cowboy boots, leather pants, and fringed jacket. He strummed a little on the electric guitar slung around his neck.

"I hope we don't have to play at all," said Velma miserably. She stood near the microphone wearing oversized glasses, tall white platform shoes, and a feather boa around her neck.

Daphne looked surprised. "I thought you loved to sing!" She was seated at the keyboards in a long, flowing dress, a wild red wig, and gobs of makeup.

"Not in front of so many people," Velma admitted. "I get stage fright."

"Well, I get vampire fright," said Shaggy, who was decked out in a fuzzy, full-length neon-green overcoat and a backward baseball cap. He plucked the strings of his bass guitar. "Like, what do you say we go on tour somewhere far, far away?"

Scooby hit the drums in agreement. He was looking totally cool in leather gloves, sunglasses, and a beret. His yellow-and-black-striped turtleneck sweater made him look like a groovy oversized bumblebee.

Meanwhile, Daphne had noticed something across the stage. She knelt down near the light fixture Matt Marvelous had grabbed before he was kidnapped. "Hey," she said, "look at this!" There was a smudge of white goo on the fixture. She stuck her finger into it and rubbed it around a little. "It's stage makeup," she told Velma, who had come over for a closer look. "So the audience can see you better." She thought for a second. "I can't imagine Matt Marvelous wearing this glowing white color."

Fred was kneeling down near the keyboards. "And look at this!" he said. "It's the print from the heel of a boot." He ran his hand over it. "That's strange," he said. "The print is sticky, like glue. But it's not glue, exactly. I don't know what it is."

Just then, Jasper and the Bad Omens showed up. Jasper, who was riding in a golf cart, watched Shaggy hopping around holding his hurt foot. "You're the new competition?" he asked, looking over the gang's costumes.

Fred nodded. "We're taking Matt Marvelous's place in the contest."

King, Queen, and Jack looked at the gang, then at one another. All three of them cracked up.

Velma tried to ignore their laughter. "You must be Jasper Ridgeway — and the Bad Omens."

"Russell warned — I mean, told us about you," Daphne added.

King was staring at Scooby. "Who ever heard of a band with a dog in it?" he sneered.

"Rog?" Scooby looked around.

Queen sniffed and tossed her hair back. "Why don't you amateurs take a break?"

"It's time for a *real* band to play," said Jack.

Fred looked disgusted. "Let's go, gang. We need to set up camp for the night, anyway."

Jasper wiped his brow with a silk handkerchief. "Camping?" he asked. "How primitive. I choose to travel in a fully furnished air-conditioned trailer myself."

Velma decided to do some investigating. "Russell told us about another band you used to manage, Wildwind," she said.

Jasper nodded. "Yes." He sighed dramatically. "They were true superstars. I had such high hopes for them, until that fateful night last year." He put his head down on the steering wheel of his golf cart. "I don't like to talk about it," he said, choking up a little. "It's just too upsetting."

"Oh, brother," muttered Fred.

"He really lays it on thick," whispered Velma.

Jasper straightened up and started his cart's engine. "Well," he said, "back to the trailer! I can't take this heat any longer." He turned to the Bad Omens. "Enjoy your rehearsal!" Then he sputtered away, leaving a big plume of smelly black smoke.

Fred coughed. "Well, nice to meet you, too!" he said.

"Let's get out of these costumes and start looking for clues," said Velma.

Chapter 8

A little while later, the gang headed for the campground. They walked past eucalyptus trees and big boulders.

"I think we may have just met our so-called vampires," Fred said thoughtfully.

"The Bad Omens?" Velma asked.

"Exactly." Fred nodded. "Jasper Ridgeway seems like the kind of guy who'd do anything to have his band win."

"So, you think he put them up to it?" Velma asked as they began to walk past the concession stand area. Delicious smells filled the air from booths selling Australian specialties like Aussie meat pie, shrimp on the barbie, and shearer's stew.

Distracted, Shaggy and Scooby slowed down to check out the food. But the rest of the gang was still talking about the mystery. "The makeup the Bad Omens were wearing looks just like the stage makeup I found," Daphne said.

"Hmm," said Velma. "Maybe we should talk to Daniel and Russell and find out more about them."

Daphne had other ideas. "I bet Jasper's trailer could tell us a thing or two."

Fred agreed. "Let's check it out. Shaggy and Scooby, you see what you can dig up around here."

Shaggy looked at Scooby. Scooby looked at Shaggy. Then they looked around at the concession stands. Both of them smiled. "Like, we'll leave no snow cone — I mean, stone — unturned!" Shaggy promised.

Fred, Velma, and Daphne stopped at the Mystery Machine to change and pick up Velma's camera. A few moments later, they headed for Jasper's fancy, streamlined trailer, which was parked near a dramatic rock formation.

"Wow," Daphne said when she saw it. "Jasper wasn't kidding when he said he travels in style."

"We've got to get a look inside," said Fred.

"How are we going to do that, Freddie?" Daphne asked.

He thought for a second. "We've got to lure him out," he answered. "And I've got a plan."

"Fred?" Velma asked.

"Wait," said Fred, holding up a hand. "This is brilliant. I'm going to go over into those bushes and imitate the call of the wild kookaburra."

"But Fred," Velma said.

"Hold on, Velma!" Fred interrupted. "I'm on a roll. Now Daphne, I want you to disguise yourself as an Aboriginal medicine woman, and —"

"Fred!" Velma shouted from where she was now standing — in the wide-open door of the trailer.

"What?"

"Or, we could just use the front door," Velma said, motioning to him and Daphne.

"Or that," said Fred. He and Daphne joined Velma and headed into the trailer.

Inside, Fred, Velma, and Daphne checked out the decor. The place was decorated '70s-style, with lava lamps, beanbag chairs, black-light posters, and an egg-shaped stereo chair.

"This is better than a museum!" said Velma, snapping a picture.

"Wow," Daphne agreed, bouncing on the waterbed. "Totally retro."

Velma checked out a framed picture showing Jasper with the members of Wildwind. "Well, Wildwind was a retro band. And everything in here is in that style."

"Seems like Jasper can't let go of the past," Daphne said.

Fred looked out the window. "C'mon, girls," he said. "We've got to work fast. Jasper could show up at any minute."

Daphne looked around. "There's so much stuff in here it's going to be hard to tell the clues from the collectibles."

"I think I've already found one!" Velma called, pulling a costume out of a dresser drawer. "This looks exactly like the costume Dark Skull is wearing in that poster!"

"Great work," Fred said. He looked into the drawer. "The costumes for Stormy Weathers and Lightning Strikes are in here, too."

"So," Velma said. "Jasper Ridgeway has reproductions of all the Wildwind costumes. Interesting."

It was time to get out of Jasper's trailer, but before they left Velma took a picture of Daphne holding the Dark Skull costume.

Chapter 9

Meanwhile, Shaggy and Scooby were digging into an awesome Australian snack of bread smeared with jam. "They call this damper bread," said Shaggy. "Like, it's sure not putting a damper on my appetite!"

Scooby just nodded. He couldn't talk because his mouth was too full. Then he took a major slurp of his drink, emptying the whole cup in one gulp.

"Like, what's next, buddy?" Shaggy asked.

Scooby didn't answer. He was staring over Shaggy's shoulder. "Rampires!"

Shaggy turned around just in time to see the three Wildwind vampires standing behind him, their fangs bared and their eyes glowing like red coals. "Zoinks!" he said. "Like, now I'm not hungry at all! Let's get out of here!" He threw down his bread and started running.

The vampires chased Shaggy and Scooby all over the concession area. They raced through an Italian food booth, where Scooby and Shaggy served them

spaghetti. Then the vampires followed the two buddies into a hall of mirrors — where the three creatures looked even bigger and scarier than ever!
Finally, Scooby and Shaggy thought they'd trapped
the vampires in tanning beds — but soon they were
on the hunt again. This time they chased Shaggy and
Scooby right up onto the stage, where the Bad
Omens were practicing a song. Shaggy ducked into
Jack's biggest drum, and Scooby squeezed in beside
him.

"What the — ?" Jack asked, just as a swirling cloud
of smoke descended onto the stage. It took the shape
of the Yowie Yahoo! It was enormous and just as terrifying as ever! Even the Bad Omens looked frightened. Then the Wildwind vampires appeared and
started fighting with the Bad Omens.

Dark Skull broke King's guitar in half and grabbed
him.

Lightning Strikes came flying toward Jack. Jack
threw his drumsticks and cymbals at him. Lightning
Strikes crashed right into the drumset and sent
pieces of it flying all over the stage.

The drum Scooby and Shaggy were hiding in
rolled to a far corner of the stage. They lifted one
edge and peered out, just in time to see Stormy
Weathers block Queen from running off the stage.
Another dark billow of smoke overtook the stage,

and Shaggy and Scooby let the drum fall back down, hiding them completely.

A moment later, Fred, Daphne, and Velma showed up. The stage was a total wreck, with pieces of guitars and drums everywhere and smoke still lingering in the air. "What happened here?" asked Fred, looking around.

"And what's with all this smoke?" Daphne asked, coughing.

"It burns my eyes," Fred said, trying to wave it away.

"And it smells so sweet — like cotton candy," said Velma.

"Cotton candy?!" exclaimed Shaggy and Scooby in unison, popping out of the drum they were still hiding in.

"Shaggy? And Scooby?" said Fred.

"What happened to the Bad Omens?" Velma asked them.

Shaggy still looked terrified. "Like, those Wildwind vampires showed up and band-napped them. Scoob and I thought we were next."

Scooby nodded, whimpering.

"Hmm," said Fred. "There go our prime suspects."

"You actually saw the vampires, Shaggy?" Velma asked.

"Ruh-huh," said Scooby.

"We both did," said Shaggy.

"What did they look like?" Fred asked.

Shaggy pointed to the poster of Wildwind. "Exactly like the guys on that poster — only much scarier. And, like, they had those creepy red eyes."

"Reah," Scooby agreed. "Red."

"Whoever it was," Fred told him, "they kidnapped the Bad Omens."

Jasper putted up in his golf cart just in time to hear that. "Kidnapped?" he asked. "Not again! The Bad Omens *can't* be kidnapped. They have to win the contest."

"Like, it's a good thing you weren't here, Jasper," Shaggy told him. "Those vampires would have flown off with you, too."

Jasper climbed out of his golf cart. "I wish they had," he wailed dramatically. "Now I'll be plagued by guilt. I should have stayed with my band instead of going back to my trailer."

Fred shot a suspicious look at Jasper. "Trailer?" he muttered. "Hmmm."

"What happened here?" asked Daniel, approaching the gang.

"My band is gone. What are we going to do?" Jasper moaned.

"There's strength in numbers," Fred said. "Let's get the Hex Girls and Russell and camp in one group."

"Russell already went home," Daniel reported. "Along with all the other festival staff."

Shaggy shivered. "Like, I wish I could say the same thing."

Jasper still wasn't convinced. "What if the vampires come while we're all sleeping?"

"We can take turns standing watch," Velma suggested.

Fred looked over at Shaggy and Scooby. "And you guys have the first tour of duty," he said. Shaggy looked scared. He and Scooby tried to tiptoe away, but Fred grabbed them. "Which starts *now*," he added.

Shaggy and Scooby were still struggling to escape. Velma held out a box of Scooby Snacks. "Would you each do it for a Scooby Snack?" she asked.

Daphne took the box from Velma. "Or maybe *two* Scooby Snacks?" she asked.

"Well," said Shaggy, "there might be room in my tummy for a Scooby Snack or two. How about you, Scooby?"

"Reah! Reah!" Scooby said, nodding hard.

Daphne and Velma tossed them their snacks. Then

Shaggy and Scooby stood at attention, ready to stand guard. "Like, everybody get some rest," Shaggy said, saluting, "because you're being watched over by the best!"

Chapter 10

Just before sunrise everybody was asleep — *including* Scooby and Shaggy. Then the drone of roaring engines started to drown out their snoring. Shaggy and Scooby woke up just in time to see bright lights coming closer. "Zoinks! Not again. Like, it's the vampires!" yelled Shaggy.

He and Scooby scrambled up a tree and looked down as the lights approached. Finally, they could see what it was: two motorcycles.

"The vampires are in a motorcycle gang?" Shaggy asked. He leaned out of the tree and the branch broke, sending him and Scooby tumbling to the ground. They landed in front of the bikers, who were wearing ripped blue jeans and leather biker jackets.

"You're not vampires," Shaggy said, looking up at them. "Like, who are you?"

"Two Skinny Dudes," answered Harry, who had bright pink hair.

Shaggy got up and looked down at his own skinny body. "Like, me, too!" he said.

"No," said Barry, who wore his hair under a black head band. "We're the band Two Skinny Dudes. I'm Barry and this is my brother, Harry."

By then, the others were awake and crawling out of their tents. "What's going on?" Fred asked.

Daniel came over to shake Harry's and Barry's hands. "Finally," he said. "I've heard so much about you from Russell. Glad you made it here all right."

"Why wouldn't we?" asked Harry.

"Some of the other bands have been kidnapped," Daniel told him.

"By vampires," Shaggy added.

Barry and Harry looked at each other and laughed.

But Fred squinted at them suspiciously. "If you weren't kidnapped, where have you been?"

Barry pulled his knapsack off his motorcycle and showed them all the camping gear inside. "Exploring Vampire Rock," he said. "We liked it so much we decided to camp up there."

"But we didn't see a single vampire," Harry told them.

"Matt Marvelous and the Bad Omens sure did," Velma said.

"And all the other finalists got so scared they drove back to Sydney," Daniel reported.

"So we're the only ones left?" Barry asked.

Harry looked excited. "Does this mean we win the contest?"

"Not quite," said Daniel. "We had a last-minute entry." He looked over at Scooby and Shaggy, who pulled out a harmonica and banjo and started playing.

Barry and Harry checked out the competition. They did not seem impressed.

Just then, the door of Jasper's trailer opened, and he came out rubbing his eyes. "What's all the racket?" he asked. "Did you find my band?"

"No, but we found another one," Daniel said. "Meet Two Skinny Dudes."

"Ah," said Jasper, shaking hands with Barry and Harry. "Russell tells me you're the next big thing. You boys have a manager?"

"No," said Harry.

Jasper smiled. He put a hand on each of Harry's and Barry's shoulders and walked them toward his trailer. "Groovy, groovy," he said. "Why don't you come into my trailer and let me tell you what I can do for your careers?" He led them right into his trailer and slammed the door.

"Jeepers," said Daphne. "He works fast."

"Hmm," Velma commented, "Jasper seemed to forget about the Bad Omens pretty quickly."

The sun was coming up by then. "We should get going," said Daniel. "We've still got two missing bands out there, and the concert starts tonight at six."

Just then, the Hex Girls stuck their heads out of their tent.

"What's with all the noise?" Thorn asked.

"How are we supposed to rest for tonight?" demanded Dusk.

"In other words, would you mind?" said Luna. The three girls disappeared inside their tent again.

Scooby and Shaggy looked at each other.

"Divas," said Shaggy, shrugging.

Chapter 11

Daniel and the gang hopped into the Mystery Machine to pay a visit to Malcolm. Daniel thought his grandfather might be able to tell them more about the Yowie Yahoo, since Malcolm knew all the local legends.

On the way to Malcolm's, Velma surfed the Internet, looking for information on vampires. "Let's see," she said, reading off the screen. "Vampires hate sunlight, they can't cross running water, and — get this! — the more people a vampire puts under his control, the greater his power becomes."

"That would explain why the Yowie Yahoo is sending Wildwind to kidnap people," Daphne said. "That is, if you believe he's real."

"Hmm," Velma went on, glancing at the Polaroid camera on the seat next to her, "it also says that vampires don't appear on film when their pictures are taken."

"Like, maybe they're just camera shy," Shaggy

said, grabbing the camera to take a picture of himself and Scooby.

Just then, the Mystery Machine pulled up to Malcolm's house. It was right on the shores of Wallaby Springs, a stream that went all the way to Vampire Rock. Malcolm had a big bonfire going. He was fanning the smoke carefully, sending up round puffs of it into the sky.

Daniel introduced the gang and told Malcolm they were here to help track down the kidnapped bands.

Shaggy was curious about what Malcolm was doing. "Like, what's the deal with the smoke signals?"

"I'm letting people know about a tribal council meeting," Malcolm explained.

Daniel rolled his eyes. "You could just use the phone, Grandfather," he said.

"The smoke smells really good," Fred commented. "What are you burning?"

"Wood from the red gum tree," Malcolm said. "We use its flowers to make honey." He pointed to a nearby tree that was covered in blooms. Scooby went over to investigate. A koala up in the tree started throwing leaves and sticks at him, but when Scooby tried to get away he discovered that his paws were stuck to the tree. When he finally pried himself loose, he flew into the stream and got soaked! But Scooby just giggled. When he finally got loose, he went over to the stream to wash off his paws.

The rest of the gang, Daniel, and Malcolm joined him there. Everybody piled into two canoes for a trip downstream. It felt good to be on the water, with the hot outback sun beating down on them. While they paddled, the gang asked Malcolm questions about the Yowie Yahoo.

He said Wildwind had been foolish to go up to Vampire Rock after dark. "They were easy prey for the Yowie Yahoo, just like all the people attending the festival will be," he said.

"So, like, what can we do to keep him and his rock star pals away?" Shaggy asked.

"According to legend," Malcolm said, "the only thing that can destroy a vampire is sunlight. But it's also believed they fear dingoes."

Shaggy thought Scooby should talk to his dingo friends about helping out, but Malcolm said dingoes were wild dogs and weren't concerned with helping humans.

While he was talking, a monstrous crocodile surfaced near Scooby and Shaggy's canoe. It opened wide and snapped its sharp teeth at Scooby's paws, just missing. "Like, that crocodile almost had his own Scooby Snack!" Shaggy said.

"Thank goodness he didn't," Daniel said. "I scheduled your group to perform tonight, right after the Hex Girls."

Velma gulped. Daphne invited Malcolm to come, but he patted her hand and said he couldn't. "Not when I believe the festival shouldn't take place at all," he said, loudly enough for Daniel to hear.

"I know how you feel, Grandfather," said Daniel. "But I've got a show to do."

Just then, Shaggy looked up. "Smoke," he said, pointing at the sky over Vampire Rock.

"They are answering my signals," said Malcolm.

"Can you show me how you do that?" asked Shaggy. "Like, if the vampires come back, I want to send an SOS: Save Our Shaggy!"

Chapter 12

"**Y**EAHHH!" The crowd roared as the Hex Girls rocked out on stage. Beams of light played over the audience as Luna, Thorn, and Dusk ripped into their first song.

The festival had begun.

The gang stood backstage with Daniel, watching. Velma was snapping pictures, trying to capture the atmosphere and the energy on stage.

Suddenly, Fred started to rub his eyes. "Man," he said, "my eyes are really burning." Then he looked up, and his jaw dropped. It looked like the Yowie Yahoo.

A menacing swirl of dark smoke hovered over the stage. Then, as the gang watched, it transformed into the three Wildwind vampires! They flew down to the stage, swirling around the Hex Girls.

"No!" cried Daniel. "Not now!"

"Jinkies!" Velma yelled, snapping a picture. "There really is a Yowie Yahoo!"

Thorn turned to Dark Skull, who was standing

right next to her. "Hey," she said. "You're ruining our encore!"

Fred and Daniel started to run toward the stage, just as the Wildwind vampires flew off, carrying the Hex Girls with them. In an instant, they had all disappeared in a cloud of smoke.

The crowd just cheered. They thought it was all part of the act.

Daphne watched as the dark smudge moved off. "Now what?" she asked.

"They must be heading to Vampire Rock," said Velma.

Fred started walking offstage. "We have to go after them," he said.

"Great idea, Fred," said Shaggy. "Follow them back to vampire central? While you're gone, Scoob and I will stay here and practice our number." He and Scooby started playing — until Shaggy broke a guitar string.

The crowd had stopped cheering by then. They stared at Shaggy and Scooby. Daniel walked over to the microphone. "Uh, weren't the Hex Girls terrific?" he said, as if everything were normal. "We'll be taking a short break. See you soon!"

There were a few boos from the crowd, but Daniel ignored them, walking over to join the gang. "Maybe my grandfather was right," he said. "Where's Russell? We have to cancel the rest of the show."

Fred calmed him down. "Not yet," he told Daniel. "I've got a plan that will end this once and for all. Now, here's what we do . . ."

Chapter 13

A little while later, the gang crossed the rickety old bridge over Wallaby Springs, just a short distance away from Vampire Rock. The massive formation loomed over them, making them feel tiny in comparison.

Daphne stared up at it. "Jeepers," she said. "I knew Vampire Rock was big, but not this big!"

"It's going to be harder than we thought to find the Hex Girls," Velma admitted.

"We need to split up," said Fred. "Daphne, Velma, and I will head this way" — he pointed — "and Shaggy and Scooby can circle around in the other direction."

Shaggy put an arm around Daphne. "Vacation has really brought us closer together," he said, trying to stall. "Like, it's a shame to split up now!"

It didn't work. Fred, Daphne, and Velma took off, leaving Shaggy and Scooby alone near the bridge. As the three of them walked around Vampire Rock, Velma knocked on the towering stone walls. "Vampire Rock seems to be just that," she said. "Solid rock."

"There's got to be a way in somehow," Fred said, just as Daphne leaned against the side of the rock, hitting a hidden switch. A door slid open and Daphne fell right in!

"You were saying?" she asked, when she popped back out, dusting herself off.

The three of them looked at one another, nodded, and stepped inside the gigantic rock. Fred took out his flashlight and used it to guide them through the dark cavern. "Secret passages always lead somewhere," he said as they worked their way upward.

Velma reached over and clicked off his flashlight. "Hmm," she said. "We should be experiencing total cave darkness right now, but we're not. So —"

"There must be light coming from inside the cave!" Fred finished her thought.

"Over there," said Daphne, pointing to a big black tarp covering the entrance to another cavern.

The three of them tiptoed over, pulled the tarp aside, and took a look. Inside, some camping lanterns cast a dim light over a clutter of equipment: several giant fans, some big lights, and a few amplifiers. Large tarps covered piles of other equipment.

"Wow," said Daphne, taking it all in. "I was expecting a vampire's lair to be, well, spookier!"

"It's more like an underground warehouse," Fred agreed.

Velma walked over to one of the lanterns. "These lanterns didn't light themselves," she said thoughtfully.

"That's right, Velma," Fred said, joining her. "They're only big enough to hold a few hours' worth of oil."

Daphne looked scared. "That means somebody was here a little while ago!"

Fred and Velma checked out the other equipment and discovered that it was still warm, as if it had been used recently. "But why?" Fred asked.

"And where?" Daphne said.

"And who?" Velma added.

The three of them continued to poke around until Daphne found another secret switch that opened up a part of the wall, exposing a big, messy bedroom with posters and graffiti on the wall, mattresses on the floor, and clothes, CDs, and books strewn all over.

"No coffins?" Daphne asked, just as the door slid shut behind her, sealing her into the bedroom. "Fred!" she called. "Velma!" Then she realized they couldn't hear her. She walked into the room, tripping over piles of clothes.

Suddenly, she found herself face-to-face with Dark Skull! He was hanging upside down, his knees wrapped around a stalactite. "Ahhhh!" Daphne screamed, running toward a light she spotted in the distance. Dark Skull did a flip, landed on his feet, and took off after her.

Daphne ran all the way to the end of a tunnel that opened out to the night sky. She peered over the edge of the opening and saw Wallaby Springs far, far below. Then she looked back. Dark Skull was still running after her.

Meanwhile, Shaggy and Scooby had walked until they found themselves back by the Wallaby Springs bridge. "Like, we've walked all the way around this creepy rock," Shaggy said, leaning against a boulder to rest. Suddenly, he heard a wild howling sound. "Like, what was that?" he asked.

Scooby shrugged nervously just as three dingoes appeared out of the dark.

Shaggy and Scooby were surrounded.

The lead dingo stared at them. His greenish-yellow eyes glowed as he growled.

"Zoinks!" said Shaggy. He looked behind him at the massive rock. He looked in front of him at the three dingoes. "We can't run," he said. "We can't climb. How are we going to get out of here?"

Scooby started digging as hard as he could.

"Good try," Shaggy told his buddy. "But we need a miracle."

Just then, Daphne did a cannonball off the cliff above them, just like the one she'd done on the cruise ship. She landed with a gigantic splash in Wallaby Springs.

A colossal wave of water soaked Scooby, Shaggy, and the dingoes. The drenched dingoes took off into the bushes.

Shaggy helped Daphne out of the water. "Like I said," he told Scooby. "A miracle. Or Daphne doing a cannonball off a cliff."

Scooby grinned and made like a judge, holding up a card that read "10."

"Thanks, guys," said Daphne, smiling.

Chapter 14

Meanwhile, Fred and Velma were still inside the secret caverns, exploring the same bedroom Daphne had found. "What a mess," said Velma, kicking aside some clothes.

"You think Daphne's in here?" asked Fred. He clicked on his flashlight and walked off to look for her. Velma walked the other way, calling for Daphne.

Suddenly, she hit her head on a stalactite. It knocked her glasses right off. "My glasses!" she cried. "Fred! Help!" She crouched down and felt around. She was still groping blindly and calling for Fred when somebody handed her the glasses. "Thanks, Freddie," she said. "I was worried there for a minute." Then she put on her glasses and realized that she was staring right at Dark Skull! "Jinkies," she said. "I take that back. *Now* I'm worried." She took off running.

She found Fred exploring another part of the vampires' sleeping quarters. "Velma!" he said when she ran up to him. "Did you find Daphne?"

She looked over her shoulder. "Wherever Daphne is," she told him, "she's a lot safer than we are."

"What do you mean?" asked Fred. Then he spotted the three Wildwind vampires running toward them. "Run!" he cried.

They ran down the corridor and leaped off the same cliff that Daphne had just dived off. "Ahhhh!" they cried as they fell into the stream.

"Fred! Velma!" Daphne cried as they climbed out dripping. "You're all right!"

"Not if we don't get out of here," said Velma, looking up at Vampire Rock.

The Wildwind vampires were swooping down toward them in a cloud of thick black smoke.

"Zoinks!" yelled Shaggy. "Like, I need a vacation from this vacation!"

"Come on!" shouted Fred. "We need to lead the vampires back to the concert and into our trap! Everybody over the bridge!"

Chapter 15

The gang ran toward the bridge. But the Wild-wind vampires swooped down in front of them, cutting them off.

They spread out so that Fred, Daphne, Velma, Shaggy, and Scooby were totally surrounded. All three vampires were grinning, their fangs glinting in the dim light.

The Yowie Yahoo towered behind them. His eyes glowed red, his fangs glistened, and his skin was deadly white against the dark night. He raised his arms and shot out fireballs in every color of the rainbow, lighting up the sky as he roared and roared again.

As far as Shaggy could tell, the only way out was to jump into Wallaby Springs. But before he could even take a step, the Yowie Yahoo started blowing fire from his mouth. The long, hot flame came way too close. Everybody ducked for cover.

The Yowie Yahoo started blowing even harder, a

hurricane of wind that knocked Scooby and Velma over. He blew harder and harder.

"Like, the Yowie Yahoo sure is full of hot air," moaned Shaggy, just as the Wildwind vampires started coming toward the gang.

The Yowie Yahoo was right above them, blowing roaring blasts of air. The vampires were coming closer. Scooby and Velma hugged each other in fear.

Then Shaggy saw something. "Look!" he yelled. "It's the dingo dogs."

Sure enough, the three wild dogs ran straight toward the vampires and chased them around the corner of Vampire Rock.

"They're getting away!" cried Daphne.

"They've got to get inside before the sun comes up," Fred explained.

"Hey Scoob, tell your cousins not to leave us here with the Yowie Yahoo," yelled Shaggy.

The Yowie Yahoo kept blowing and roaring. The gang held on for dear life. Then Fred noticed that the sun was just beginning to rise. "The vampires have to get away before the sun comes up," he said. "The Yowie Yahoo does, too."

"If he doesn't, the sun will destroy him," said Velma.

The sky grew a little brighter. Then one small ray

of light from the sun hit Scooby's collar at the perfect angle, bouncing off to hit the Yowie Yahoo right in the chest! He roared and threw fireballs from both hands.

Bang! There was a deafening explosion.

Chapter 16

The gang watched with relief as the Yowie Yahoo faded completely away.

"Scooby you did it!" cried Daphne. "You defeated the Yowie Yahoo!"

Everybody came out of their hiding places to hug Scooby.

Then the dingoes reappeared from behind Vampire Rock. The lead dingo walked right up to Scooby and held up a paw for a high five. Then they ran off, howling.

"You're an honorary dingo, Scooby!" said Velma.

"Ringo? Rooray!" Scooby said.

Daphne was still worried. "What about the Hex Girls?" she asked.

Shaggy was looking past her. "Like, we could just ask the vampires where they are," he told her, pointing.

Sure enough, the Wildwind vampires were back. And they were running straight toward the gang.

"Quick!" said Fred. "Over the bridge!"

"The sunlight destroyed the Yowie Yahoo," Daphne said as they ran. "Why isn't it destroying Wildwind?"

"You want to stop and ask them?" Fred asked.

"No, thanks!" Daphne gasped.

By then, the gang was over the bridge. "Like, we just crossed running water," Shaggy said. "The vampires shouldn't be able to follow us." Still running, he turned to look — and slammed into a tree.

Scooby ran to help him. They looked back to see the Wildwind vampires run right over the bridge, almost catching up with them.

"Didn't these vampires read the rule book?" Shaggy asked, taking off again.

He and Scooby kept running, right into the campground. Fred, Daphne, and Velma had gotten there first. "Now!" said Fred, popping up from behind a boulder as Scooby and Shaggy appeared with the vampires right behind them.

Daniel appeared from behind a bush and threw a boomerang that cut the rope holding up a big net from a tree. But Shaggy and Scooby got tangled up in the rope, and the flew up into the air.

"Oh, no!" cried Daphne.

Then the net swooped down and caught the vampires, bouncing them into the air.

Scooby stuck his tongue out at them in midair.

"Great work, Daniel," said Fred, looking at the

vampires hanging there in the net. A koala bear was throwing sticks at them.

"Yeah," Shaggy agreed. "I didn't think *anything* would stop those vampires."

"That's because they're not real vampires," Velma said. She held up the picture she'd snapped as the vampires kidnapped the Hex Girls. "If they were, they wouldn't have been captured on film."

Jasper came running up. "Jolly good work!" he shouted. "You've snared the vampires!"

"Now we can find out what happened to the bands," Daniel said.

"Right," said Velma. "At first we thought the Bad Omens were behind all this. But when they disappeared, we had to search for new suspects."

As she spoke, Fred was dragging a hose toward the net. He started spraying the two vampires whose faces showed. Their makeup washed away, revealing their real faces.

Everybody gasped.

Chapter 17

"Well, I'll be!" said Daniel. "Two Skinny Dudes!"

Sure enough, it was Harry and Barry, caught in the net!

"That's two vampires," said Daniel. "Who's the third?"

Fred untied the knot and let the net fall to the ground. Once the vampires untangled themselves, it was easy to see the third one.

"Russell!" Scooby said.

"Russell," said Daniel unbelievingly. "You were my partner! This doesn't make sense."

Russell, Barry, and Harry stood up and pulled off the netting. "Nobody say anything," Russell told Harry and Barry, before they could speak.

"That's fine," Fred said. "We can do all the talking and still get to the bottom of this mystery."

Velma stepped forward. "It took us a while to put all the pieces together," she said. "When we saw Jasper getting so chummy with Two Skinny Dudes, we thought *he* might be the third vampire."

"Me?" asked Jasper. "I could never wear all that makeup. I've got very sensitive skin." He stroked his face.

"But you did manage the Bad Omens," said Velma. "We thought you took some of their makeup so you and Two Skinny Dudes could copy Wildwind's glam-rock look."

"We also paid a visit to your trailer, but you weren't there," Fred said.

"That's not a crime!" Jasper said, holding up his hands. "Okay, okay, confession time. I wasn't in my trailer because I was meeting with the Hex Girls about being their manager. I didn't want the Bad Omens to find out."

"But," said Daphne, "that doesn't explain why you have those costumes."

"Wildwind was the greatest band I ever managed!" said Jasper. "I kept those costumes to remind me of all our good times." He sighed. "I wish I knew what happened to them."

"Why don't you ask them yourselves?" Fred asked. He, Velma, and Daphne walked toward Harry, Barry, and Russell and pulled masks off their faces to reveal different faces below.

The faces of Wildwind.

"I don't believe it!" Jasper said. "Wildwind — you're alive!"

"Okay," Shaggy whispered to Scooby. "Like, now I'm really confused."

"Re, roo," Scooby agreed.

Lightning Strikes spoke up. "We should have won that contest last year. When we didn't, we decided to disappear."

"We thought a mysterious disappearance would help our careers," explained Stormy Weathers.

"We climbed up the rock using our mountain-climbing equipment. Then we went to work inside our cave recording studio, practicing so we could make a big comeback at this year's Vampire Rock Music Festival," Lightning Strikes went on.

"But then we remembered the rules of the contest meant we couldn't enter again," Dark Skull said sadly.

Fred nodded. "That's when you came up with a way to get around those rules — and make sure you'd win this year's contest."

"With Dark Skull already posing as Russell, Stormy Weathers and Lightning Strikes became Two Skinny Dudes — an unsigned band in the contest," Daphne went on.

Velma spoke up next. "The three of you took advantage of the local legend surrounding Wildwind and disguised yourselves as vampires. You planned to kidnap all the other bands in the contest, so Two Skinny Dudes would win."

"But the crowd wouldn't see Two Skinny Dudes closing the show," Fred explained. "Instead, they would see Wildwind in their first performance since last year."

"They hoped all the attention from closing the show at Vampire Rock would make their careers take off," Velma finished.

Daniel nodded. "I'm starting to get it," he said.

Shaggy still looked totally clueless. "But, like, if they're not vampires, how did they fly?"

Scooby made flying motions. He looked just as bewildered as Shaggy.

"They used their mountain-climbing equipment," Fred explained. "They rigged it in the trees near the stage so they could swoop down and kidnap the acts."

"They used the same equipment to make it look like they were flying at Vampire Rock," Velma added.

"This is all very interesting," Jasper said, "but can somebody please tell me where the Bad Omens are?"

Fred frowned. "That's one answer we don't have."

Lightning Strikes spoke up. "We sent them and Matt Marvelous on diving trips to the Great Barrier Reef."

"All expenses paid," added Stormy Weathers. "They were thrilled."

"We didn't really kidnap anybody," Dark Skull admitted.

"What about the Hex Girls? They weren't your competition," said Velma.

"But *you* were," said Stormy Weathers.

"We knew you'd come after them, and that would give us the chance to send you on your way as well," said Dark Skull.

"Where are the Hex Girls now?" asked Fred.

"Don't worry," Thorn called from offstage. "We're fine!" She, Luna, and Dusk appeared, along with Malcolm.

"Those creepy guys took us to their hideout in Vampire Rock," said Luna.

"They offered us a free trip if we would leave the festival, but we refused," Dusk put in.

"So they took us to the Outback and left us there," Thorn said.

Fred nodded. "They knew we'd keep looking until we found you, making us miss our chance to perform."

"And leave Two Skinny Dudes as the only group left in the contest," said Daphne.

"Like, how did you find your way back here?" Shaggy asked the Hex Girls.

"Us girls can take care of ourselves," said Dusk.

"We got away," Luna said. "Then we wandered through the outback until Malcolm found us."

"The way they were dressed I thought they were vampires, too," said Malcolm.

"There are no vampires, grandfather," Daniel reminded him.

"Daniel's right, Mr. Illiwara. Wildwind is definitely human," Fred said.

"They used smoke whenever they flew so no one could see their climbing ropes. You helped us figure that out, sir," Velma explained.

"It was smoke from the red gum tree," Daphne said. "Making sweet smoke like your signals. That's how we figured it out."

Shaggy was beginning to understand. "And, like, that's why we also found a boot print made from red gum on the stage!"

Malcolm still wasn't totally convinced. "What about the Yowie Yahoo?"

"We've got an explanation for that, too," Fred answered.

Velma nodded. "Wildwind spent all of last year in Vampire Rock, perfecting their act. They're masters of special effects."

"They used a slide projector to make a giant image of the Yowie Yahoo," Fred said. "And they used their other equipment to add fire, wind, and explosions. That made it more realistic."

"So, like, because he was just a projection, the sunlight reflecting off Scooby's tag made the Yowie Yahoo disappear!" Shaggy said.

"Bingo," said Fred.

Velma scratched Scooby between the ears. "Thanks to Scooby, we were able to solve the mystery."

Malcolm looked embarrassed. "I'm sorry I let my belief in the vampire legend get in the way of your show, Daniel."

"Wildwind had us all fooled, Grandfather," said Daniel.

"And we would have gotten away with it, too," said Dark Skull. "If it weren't for you meddling kids."

Daniel turned toward the gang. "Hey," he said. "Since all the other bands in the contest are eliminated, that makes you the winner."

Velma gulped. "Does that mean what I think it means?"

Chapter 18

When night fell, the Vampire Rock Music Festival came to life once more. Daniel stood on stage facing the crowd, the curtains closed behind him. He spoke into the microphone. "And now, with a little help from their friends the Hex Girls, please welcome the Meddling Kids!"

The crowd roared as the curtain opened. Fred rocked out on guitar, Daphne played her keyboards, and Velma stood near the mike. Shaggy jumped around, playing bass, and Scooby pounded on the drums. The gang was styling in their rock star costumes. The Hex Girls were on stage, too, singing backup.

"Meddling Kids?" Daphne called over to Fred as they played the intro to their first song.

Fred shrugged. "Works for me!" he called back with a smile.

Velma started to sing. At first, she was a little shy. But the crowd seemed to like her, and soon she opened up and let it rip. She belted out the song, with the others playing hard behind her.

As the gang played, a big, bright full moon rose right over Vampire Rock. On a cliff below, the lead dingo sat staring up at the glowing globe. Then he let out a howl.

Scooby heard it. He howled back as he banged on the drums. "Scooby-Dooby-Doo!"

Scooby and the gang were heading down under for vacation in Australia! Fred, Daphne, Velma, Shaggy, and Scooby-Doo wanted to check out a music festival at the legendary Vampire Rock.

Meanwhile, the rest of the gang set a trap for the Wildwind vampires
— with a little help from Daniel and his boomerang.

The vampires turned out to be Russell and Two Skinny Dudes! They were angry that Wildwind had lost the best band contest the year before and decided to take their revenge by ruining the contest.

The gang decided to go undercover as musicians so they could look for clues. And they found plenty!

Another group, the Bad Omens, arrived with their manager, Jasper. The Bad Omens seemed like bad news — they kept making fun of the gang's stage costumes.

That night, the gang decided it was time to climb Vampire Rock and investigate.

Inside the Rock, Fred, Daphne, and Velma found lots of musical and lighting equipment...

The vampires chased Scooby and Shaggy on to the stage where the Bad Omens were rehearsing. Then the vampires' leader, the Yowie Yahoo, appeared and kidnapped the band! They all disappeared back behind Vampire Rock.

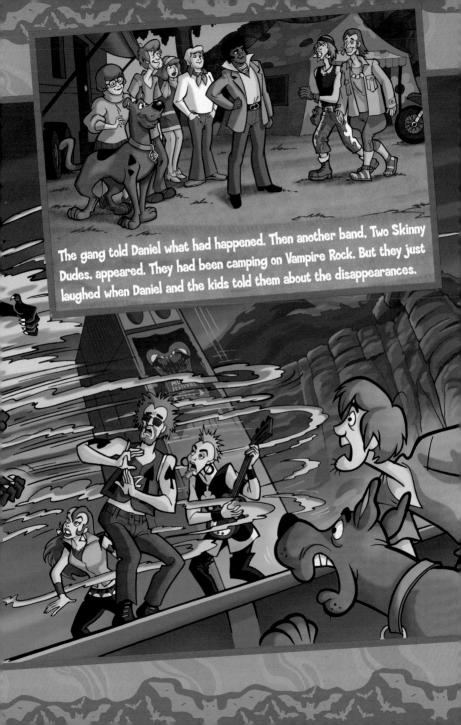

The gang told Daniel what had happened. Then another band, Two Skinny Dudes, appeared. They had been camping on Vampire Rock. But they just laughed when Daniel and the kids told them about the disappearances.

Meanwhile, Scooby and Shaggy had found Wildwind themselves! The Wildwind vampires started chasing the chums around.

Fred, Daphne, and Velma decided to search the Bad Omens' trailer for clues. They found costumes just like the ones Wildwind wore! Hmmmm...

Then the Yowie Yahoo and the Wildwind vampires appeared and started chasing the gang again! The Yowie Yahoo shot fireballs out of its mouth.

Just then, the sun began to rise! The light from the sun reflected off Scooby's dog tag and bounced onto the Yowie Yahoo — and made it disappear into thin air!

The gang arrived at Vampire Rock a bit early — and Shaggy and Scooby were terrified when they saw some dingoes howling at the rock. Like, ruh-roh!

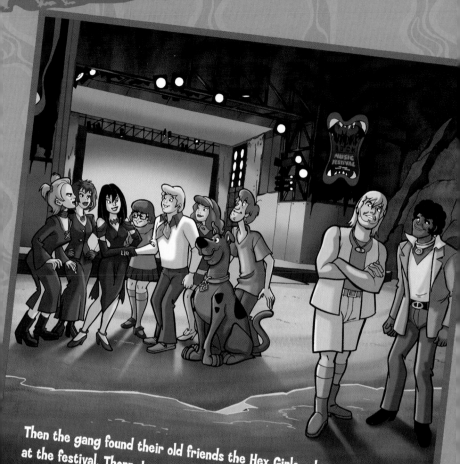

Then the gang found their old friends the Hex Girls, who were performing at the festival. Thorn, Luna, Dusk, and the concert's organizers Russell and Daniel told the gang that musicians were disappearing from Vampire Rock. And a band called Wildwind that had vanished without a trace a year ago seemed to be behind the mysterious occurrences.

Thanks to Scooby and the gang, the concert went on as planned — and the kids even got to perform! "Rooby-Dooby-Doo!" sang Scooby.